EMMA

Original story by Jane Austen
Retold by Rebecca Stevens
Series Advisor Professor Kimberley Reynolds
Illustrated by Briony May Smith

OXFORD
UNIVERSITY PRESS

Letter from the Author

I grew up in a tiny village in the middle of nowhere. There wasn't much to do so I spent a lot of time sitting up trees and dropping things on people (usually my sister because there was nobody else around). Sometimes I put on wellington boots and went for long walks in the ditches that surrounded the fields behind our house. That was when the weather was nice.

When it wasn't nice I used to read. I read anything I could get hold of: library books, fairy tales, comics, the back of the cereal packet ... Then, later on, I read *Emma*. Jane Austen wrote that Emma was 'a heroine whom no one but myself will much like.' But I liked her. I still do, actually. She's bossy and big-headed and occasionally unkind. But she's also funny and clever and she gets things wrong when she's trying to do right. And she grew up in a little village where there's not much to do. Just like me. I hope you like her too.

Rebecca Stevens

Jane Austen's World

When Jane Austen wrote *Emma* in 1815, life for girls and women was very different from how it is today. Girls hardly ever went to school. If your family had enough money, you might be educated at home by a governess, but you wouldn't study the same subjects as boys. You'd be taught to read, of course, and how to write in a beautiful script; you might learn to speak French and to play the piano or paint a pretty picture ...

But that would be it.

Then, when you got older, you wouldn't be able to go to university, and, if you came from a middle- or upper-class family, there were very few ways that you could earn your own living. If you didn't get married (preferably to someone with loads of money!) your only options were to become a governess yourself or to stay at home and depend on your family to support you.

Or ... you could write some books that become bestsellers and are loved by millions of people from all over the world for hundreds and hundreds of years.

Like Jane Austen.

Emma's family and friends

Mr Weston *Married* ------------ **Mrs Weston**

(was Miss Taylor – used to be Emma's governess)

Son from first marriage

Frank Churchill

Emma

Best friends

Robert Martin

Harriet

Mr Elton

Mr Woodhouse

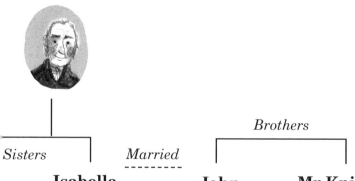

Sisters

Isabella

Married

Brothers

John Knightley

Mr Knightley

Mrs Bates

Miss Bates

Niece

Jane Fairfax

Part 1
Chapter 1
Emma

Emma's life seemed perfect. She was good-looking, everybody said so. She was clever, she knew that herself. And she was rich: the richest twenty-one-year-old in Highbury, where she lived with her father in the grandest house in the village.

But Emma Woodhouse was lonely. Her mother had died when she was little and it was seven years since her older sister Isabella had married and gone to live with her husband in London. And now Miss Taylor – the young woman who had been employed as Emma's governess and had become her best friend – had also got married. Her new home wasn't far away; Emma could visit every day if she wanted to, but she knew that things would never be the same again. The wedding was over, Miss Taylor was now Mrs Weston, and Emma was alone with her father. Who was asleep.

So she was glad when Mr Knightley arrived. He was a close friend of the family, the brother of Emma's sister's husband, and Emma was always pleased to see him, although he was nearly thirty-seven. Mr Woodhouse woke up and immediately started to talk about the wedding.

'Poor Miss Taylor! 'Tis a sad business.'

Emma's father hated change and couldn't understand why everyone else didn't hate it too. Why did Miss Taylor have to go and get married when she could have stayed with him and Emma at Hartfield House forever? It made no sense!

Mr Knightley smiled. 'Poor Miss Taylor? Poor Mr and Miss Woodhouse, if you please!'

'Yes, indeed, Mr Knightley. Dear Emma will be very sorry to lose poor Miss Taylor,' her father agreed. 'She will miss her more than she thinks.'

Emma turned her face away, caught between smiles and tears.

'I'm sure that is true, sir,' said Mr Knightley, with a quick glance at Emma. 'But Emma must be as glad as all of us to see Miss Taylor so happily married.'

'And you have forgotten one matter of joy to me,' said Emma, forcing herself to smile. 'I made the match myself!'

Mr Knightley shook his head at her.

'Everybody said Mr Weston would never marry again,' she continued. 'It was such a long time since his first wife died and he seemed so content to be single. But I did not believe it. Ever since the day four years ago when Miss Taylor and I met him in the village and he rushed away and borrowed umbrellas for us the moment it started to rain – I made up my mind: Miss Taylor and Mr Weston were going to be married!'

'You made a lucky guess,' said Mr Knightley. 'That is all.'

Emma smiled. 'And have you never known the pleasure of a lucky guess, Mr Knightley? I pity you!'

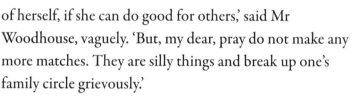

'Emma never thinks of herself, if she can do good for others,' said Mr Woodhouse, vaguely. 'But, my dear, pray do not make any more matches. They are silly things and break up one's family circle grievously.'

'Only one more, Papa.' Emma looked at them both. 'Mr Elton!'

Mr Elton was the new vicar of Highbury. He was very young, very popular and very good-looking.

'I made up my mind when I saw him at the church today. That man has been single long enough, Papa. He needs a wife!'

Mr Knightley laughed. 'Invite him to dinner, Emma,' he said. 'Serve him the best fish and chicken. But leave the man to choose his own wife.'

Emma smiled and said nothing. She didn't need to. She had, as she said, made up her mind.

All she had to do now was to find the right young lady.

Chapter 2
Harriet

Harriet Smith was a pretty blonde girl of seventeen with round blue eyes and a look of great sweetness. She had been a pupil at Mrs Goddard's boarding school in the village since she was a child and had stayed on there as she had no family of her own. Emma had known her by sight for some time.

It was only now that she began to find her truly interesting.

Harriet wasn't clever, but she was sweet and grateful and touchingly impressed with everything she saw and everybody she met, especially Miss Woodhouse. Emma found her delightful. *With just a little help,* she thought, *some gentle advice on how to behave and the sort of friends to choose, Harriet could rise above her humble background and become quite perfect. And she, Emma, would be the one to do it!* Harriet could never take Miss Taylor's place in Emma's life, but it would be an interesting and kindly enterprise that would almost make up for the loss of her best friend.

And so Emma and Harriet Smith became friends. Harriet visited Hartfield often and Emma liked her more each time. Harriet loved to talk and it amused Emma to listen as she chattered on about her concerns: Mrs Goddard, the girls at school, the teachers and – Mr Martin.

Mr Martin was a farmer, Emma learned, a young man of twenty-four who lived with his mother and two sisters just outside the village. And Harriet liked him. Harriet liked him a lot. Questions needed to be asked.

'What sort of looking man is Mr Martin?' said Emma. 'Is he handsome?'

Harriet seemed flustered. 'Oh! Not handsome, no, not *handsome*. I thought him very plain at first, but I do not think him so plain now. One does not, you know, after a time. But did you never see him, Miss Woodhouse?' she added, changing the subject rather quickly. 'He is in Highbury every now and then. I am sure we will both see him soon.'

Harriet was right. They met Mr Martin the next day when they were out walking. He was polite and respectful to Emma – and delighted to see Harriet.

Emma watched him closely. His appearance was neat and he seemed respectable enough, but he was not a gentleman. Harriet could – and would – do better!

Emma had walked on in order to leave the pair together and after only a few minutes Harriet came running up, full of smiles and blushes.

'Well, Miss Woodhouse, what do you think? Is he so very plain?'

'He is plain, undoubtedly,' said Emma. 'But that is nothing compared with his complete lack of gentility.'

Harriet's face fell. 'To be sure,' she said. 'He is not so genteel as a real gentleman.'

'Precisely,' said Emma. 'Since you've got to know us, Harriet, you have been in the company of some real gentlemen. I should be surprised if you could not see that compared to them, Mr Martin is a very inferior creature.'

'He is not like Mr Knightley, certainly.'

'Mr Knightley is not the only gentleman you have met, Harriet. What say you to ... ' (and here, Emma paused to allow her words to have their full effect) '... *Mr Elton*?'

Harriet looked flustered. 'Oh! Yes. There is a great difference between Mr Martin and Mr Elton. I see that now.'

'Mr Elton is a *real* gentleman: handsome, obliging and good-mannered. And I have noticed, Harriet,' Emma added, 'that his manners to you have been particularly obliging of late. Did I not tell you what he said of you the other day?'

Harriet blushed and smiled as Emma repeated, with only a little embellishment, some warm personal praise she had recently drawn from Mr Elton about her friend.

Emma smiled too, but only to herself. Mr Elton was the very person to drive all thoughts of the young farmer from Harriet's mind.

Chapter 3
Mr Elton

It was usually the same few people who called at Hartfield House in the evening to eat supper and play cards. Tonight it was Mr Knightley and Mr Elton, along with three ladies of the village: Mrs and Miss Bates, an elderly lady and her daughter who lived close by; and Mrs Goddard, who ran the school.

And Harriet, of course. Emma made sure of that.

'Did you ever have your portrait painted, Harriet?' she said, when there was a slight pause in the conversation.

Harriet was on the point of leaving the room and only stopped to reply innocently, 'Oh! Dear me, no, Miss Woodhouse! Never!'

As soon as she was out of sight, Emma turned to Mr Elton. 'What an exquisite possession a good portrait of her would be, Mr Elton!' she said. 'I almost long to attempt it myself.'

Emma's artistic talent was widely known and much appreciated. Her pictures of flowers, landscapes and members of the family were to be found hanging on walls all over Highbury. Her sister Isabella had even found space for one in her London house.

'It would indeed be a delight!' cried Mr Elton, with

a little too much enthusiasm. 'Let me entreat you, Miss Woodhouse, to use your considerable talent to create a likeness of your friend!'

Good man, thought Emma. *You are already halfway to being in love with her.*

'Well,' she said aloud, 'as you give me such kind encouragement, Mr Elton, I believe I shall try.'

And so it was settled. Emma produced her paints, and a smiling and blushing Harriet was persuaded to sit for her portrait, Mr Elton entertaining the guests by reading aloud from a book of poems he had brought along especially.

Everybody who saw the finished work liked it very much, but Mr Elton was in raptures.

'I never saw such a likeness!' he exclaimed. 'It is perfect, Miss Woodhouse! Quite, quite perfect!'

'You have made her too tall, Emma,' said Mr Knightley.

Emma knew this was true but she was not going to admit it.

'It is very pretty, my dear,' said Mr Woodhouse, 'but there is one thing I do not like. She seems to be sitting outside with only a little shawl over her shoulders – it makes me think she will catch cold.'

'I cannot agree, sir!' cried Mr Elton. 'The picture is perfect! Oh, I cannot take my eyes from it!'

The next thing was to get the picture framed, a service

that Mr Elton was only too happy to perform. He would take it to London, he would choose the frame, he would return it to the artist without delay! Oh, it was impossible to say how gratified he would be to be entrusted with such an errand!

Emma was content. Her picture was a success and her friend appeared to have made exactly the right impression upon Mr Elton. Everything was working out exactly as she had planned.

And then the letter arrived.

Chapter 4
The Letter

The letter was from Mr Martin. It had been left for Harriet at Mrs Goddard's while she was out and it contained a proposal of marriage.

Harriet arrived, letter in hand, in a perfect frenzy of agitation.

'Who could have thought it?' Harriet cried. 'Will you read it? Pray do, Miss Woodhouse. And then tell me what to do.'

Emma did not need to be asked twice. She read the letter and was surprised. It was well written. There were no grammatical errors or spelling mistakes and it was admirably brief and to the point. It would not have disgraced a gentleman.

Harriet was watching her face. 'Well?' she said. 'Is it a good letter, Miss Woodhouse? Or do you think it too short?'

Emma took a deep breath. 'It is a very good letter,' she said. 'So good that I think one of Mr Martin's sisters must have helped him write it.'

'Oh! But what shall I do? Miss Woodhouse, you must help me! Tell me what to do!'

'My dear Harriet, you must answer it, of course –

and speedily.'

'But what shall I say? Miss Woodhouse! Please advise me!'

'Oh no, no, no. Your reply must be your own work, Harriet. I know you will make yourself perfectly clear, for there must be no room for any doubt. You will thank Mr Martin for his kind offer and express your sorrow for the disappointment and pain it is your sad duty to inflict upon him.'

Harriet's face fell. 'You think I ought to refuse him.'

'You surely don't mean to accept him? Harriet?'

'No! I mean – yes! I mean – oh, I don't know! Dear Miss Woodhouse, tell me what to do!'

Emma was firm. 'No, Harriet. This is something you must settle with your own feelings.'

Harriet looked down at the letter. 'I had no idea he liked me so much,' she said quietly.

Emma thought quickly. 'I lay it down as a general rule,' she said, 'that if a woman is not *completely* sure whether to accept a man, then she ought to refuse him.'

'You think I had better say no?'

'That is for you to decide, Harriet,' said Emma. 'If you are quite certain that you prefer Mr Martin to every other man that you have ever been in company with, then you must not hesitate. But ... '

Emma paused. Harriet turned away, biting her lip.

'Be honest with yourself, Harriet. It would not be a kindness to accept Mr Martin out of pity. Is there no one else you have been thinking of? Someone, perhaps, whose name begins with an E?'

There was a long pause while Harriet twisted the letter in her hands. Eventually, she said, 'Miss Woodhouse. As you will not give me your opinion, I must make up my own mind. And I have decided – I am really almost nearly completely determined that – I will refuse Mr Martin.'

She looked at her friend, her round blue eyes shining with what looked like tears. 'Miss Woodhouse? Do you think I am right?'

Emma looked back at her little friend's pleading face and smiled. 'Perfectly, perfectly right, my dearest Harriet. And now – to write your reply!'

Chapter 5
The Argument

So the letter was written, sealed and sent. Emma was pleased with her work, but the next day, Harriet seemed rather low.

'Now he has got my letter,' she said, 'I wonder what he is doing. Oh, I hope he will not mind too much.'

'Let us think of more cheerful matters!' said Emma. 'Consider, Harriet, at this very moment, *Mr Elton* may be showing your portrait around and saying how much more beautiful you are than your picture!'

Harriet blushed and smiled, and Emma was pleased to observe that she went away to Mrs Goddard's looking much more cheerful than before.

Mr Knightley called soon afterwards and straight away began speaking of Harriet. 'She is a pretty little creature,' he said, 'and in good hands will turn out to be a valuable woman.'

Emma was pleased. 'I am glad you think so, Mr Knightley. I take that as a great compliment to me as much as to my friend. But you look as if you have some news you are bursting to share.'

'I have indeed,' said Mr Knightley. He was trying not to smile. 'I have reason to believe,' he went on, with an air of importance, 'that your little friend Harriet will soon hear something to her advantage. An offer of marriage, no less.'

Emma could not believe her ears. Had Mr Elton confided in Mr Knightley? Was it possible that her plan was working so soon?

She took a deep breath, determined to remain calm.

'Indeed?' she said. 'And who, may I ask – ?'

'Robert Martin is the man.'

Emma could not believe her ears. 'Robert Martin?'

'Indeed. He told me himself, Emma. He is desperately in love and means to make her an offer within the next few days.'

There was a small pause. Emma was beginning to enjoy herself.

'I will tell you something, Mr Knightley,' she said, 'in return for what you have told me. Mr Martin has already spoken to Harriet. He wrote to her yesterday. And was refused.'

'*What?*'

Emma was obliged to repeat her statement before it was believed.

'Harriet Smith refused Robert Martin?'

Emma inclined her head. 'I believe that is what I said.'

Mr Knightley stood up, quite red with indignation and surprise. 'Then she is a greater simpleton than I thought! What is the foolish girl about?'

'Oh! To be sure,' cried Emma. 'A man can never understand why a woman would refuse an offer of marriage. He always imagines she must be ready for anybody who asks her.'

'Nonsense! A man imagines no such thing! But what is the meaning of this, Emma? Harriet Smith refused Robert Martin? You must be mistaken!'

'I saw her answer, Mr Knightley. Nothing could be clearer.'

'You saw her answer? You *wrote* her answer! Emma, this is your doing! You persuaded her to refuse him.'

'And if I did? Mr Martin is a very respectable young man but he is not Harriet's equal. He is just a farmer.'

'A respectable, intelligent, gentleman-farmer! Who would not have proposed unless he was sure his affection was returned! He loves her, Emma! And he believes that she loves him!'

Emma was beginning to feel uncomfortable.

'Emma, you have not been a good friend to Harriet Smith,' continued Mr Knightley. 'She has no money of her own, and no family. She will not get a better offer of marriage, you may depend upon it.'

'I cannot agree. Harriet is not clever, I admit, but she has a better sense than you are aware of, and a girl of such loveliness and sweetness of manner is certain to be admired by men with better prospects than Mr Robert Martin.'

Mr Knightley looked at her sharply. 'I know your love of matchmaking, Emma. And I warn you, as a friend, that if it is Elton you have set your heart on for Harriet, then you should think again.'

Emma laughed and denied it.

'Trust me, Emma. Elton will not do. He is far too interested in a comfortable life to throw himself away on a young girl who has nothing but a pretty face to recommend her.'

'I am very obliged to you,' said Emma, laughing again. 'If I had set my heart on Mr Elton marrying Harriet, it would be kind of you to open my eyes. But at present I only want to keep Harriet to myself.'

And that was that. They parted on bad terms, both of them equally sure they were right, but only one of them perfectly determined to prove it.

Chapter 6
The Vicarage

As November turned to December, Emma was pleased to see that Harriet appeared to think less and less of Mr Martin and more and more of Mr Elton. The weather was still fine enough for the two young ladies to take their regular walks, and Emma decided to use one of these to further her plans for her friend.

It was as they were passing the vicarage, Mr Elton's house, that Emma stopped.

'There it is, Harriet. Mr Elton's residence.'

'Oh! What a sweet house!' said Harriet. 'How very beautiful! There are the yellow curtains that Mrs Goddard admires so much!'

Emma did not think the house beautiful and found the curtains of a very inferior quality. But she held her tongue. 'Indeed, my dear Harriet. And who knows? One day, that sweet house may be your home too!'

Harriet blushed, but before she could reply the gentleman himself appeared. Emma immediately contrived to leave the two alone. She stopped, pretending to adjust the lace of one of her boots, and begged them to walk on ahead.

They did so, and Emma was pleased to see that they

were soon engaged in lively conversation. She was less pleased, however, when she caught up with them. Mr Elton was giving Harriet an account of the party he had attended the night before at a friend's house.

'There was cheese!' he was saying. 'Oh, a fine selection, Miss Smith. Stilton, North Wiltshire, Wensleydale. And celery! Oh, there was plenty of celery. Beetroot ... '

Anything is interesting between those in love, Emma told herself. *And if I had only stayed away longer the conversation would soon have moved on to other matters.*

As she was considering this, another idea came to her. Knowing how Harriet longed to see inside the house, she stooped down again and, while the couple's attention was elsewhere, broke her bootlace. Then, straightening up: 'Part of my lace is gone! Oh, Mr Elton, I must beg leave to stop at your house and ask your housekeeper for a bit of ribbon or string to keep my boot from falling off.'

Mr Elton seemed overcome at the idea and immediately conducted them inside. Emma passed through to the back with the housekeeper, leaving the lovers alone.

Now, she thought, *surely now, the gentleman will declare himself.*

But it was not to be. Emma spent as long as she could with the housekeeper but she could not stay in the back room forever. When she rejoined them, the lovers were standing close together at one of the windows. For half a minute Emma thought her scheme had been a success. But no. Mr Elton had been most friendly, most gentleman-like. He had told Harriet he had seen them walk by, he admitted he had purposefully followed them. But that was all.

Ah well, thought Emma, *at least there had been no further talk of cheese.*

Chapter 7
The Carriage Ride

Christmas was coming and everyone was invited to dine at Mr and Mrs Weston's house. Emma had hoped it would be another opportunity for Harriet to spend time with Mr Elton, but it was not to be. Her friend had fallen ill with a cold and was unable to go.

Poor Mr Elton, Emma thought to herself. *To miss an opportunity to spend another evening with the lovely Miss Smith! How disappointed he will be!*

Mr Elton did not seem disappointed. When Emma's carriage stopped for him outside the vicarage, he was inside instantly, very smart and smiling and less concerned about Harriet's cold than he was about the possibility of Emma catching it.

'A sore throat?' he cried, when Emma brought up the subject. 'I hope not infectious! You should take care of yourself as well as your friend, Miss Woodhouse. Let me entreat you to run no risks.'

His concern was so overwhelming that Emma was glad when the journey was over and they were safely installed with the other guests in Mrs Weston's drawing room.

It was the first time she and Mr Knightley had met since their quarrel and Emma was hoping they might be friends again. *She* had not been in the wrong, she knew that, and *he* would not admit he had been, but it was time to forget their differences.

Before she got the chance to speak to Mr Knightley, however, Emma was drawn aside by Mrs Weston. And Mr Elton's odd behaviour did not stop. Whilst she and her old friend were sitting together, enjoying their first proper conversation for a long time, he would constantly appear at her elbow to interrupt their talk: Was Emma warm enough? Would she be more comfortable nearer the fire? Was she sure she wasn't sitting in a draught? Emma was relieved when the party moved through to dinner and she found herself seated at the other end of the table, next to Mr Weston.

'We want only two guests more to be just the right number!' he said, smiling. 'Your pretty little friend, Miss Smith, and my son, Frank.'

Frank Churchill. There was something in the name, in the very *idea* of Mr Weston's son by his first marriage, that had always interested Emma. After his mother died, Frank had been adopted by his uncle and his wife, a wealthy couple with no children of their own. He was now twenty-three years old and said to be *very* handsome. Emma had never met him but she had often thought – especially since his father's marriage to her best friend – that if she *were* to marry (which of course she wasn't), he was the very person to suit her in age, character and condition. And she suspected that Mr and Mrs Weston thought the same.

'Did you hear me telling the others,' Mr Weston was saying, 'that we are expecting Frank within a fortnight?'

So Frank Churchill was to visit Highbury at last! The news put Emma in such good spirits that she quite forgot Mr Elton ... until it was time to go and she was once again alone in the carriage with him.

They had scarcely turned onto the road when she found her hand seized, her attention demanded and Mr Elton loudly declaring his love. She tried to stop him but he would go on – hoping – fearing – adoring – ready to die if she refused him. He was sure, he said, that she was aware of his love. He was convinced she would accept him.

Emma decided to pretend he wasn't serious.

'Mr Elton!' she cried. 'I am very much astonished – this to *me*! You must take me for my friend!'

'Your friend?'

'Yes! Any message to Miss Smith I shall be happy to deliver. But please, Mr Elton, no more of this to *me*!'

'Miss Smith? *Message to Miss Smith?*' Mr Elton was confused. What could she possibly mean? It was Emma he loved, Emma he worshipped, Emma he intended to marry!

The object of Mr Elton's adoration took a deep breath. 'Mr Elton. My astonishment is beyond anything I can express. After all your attentions to Miss Smith – to be addressing *me* in this manner.'

'Miss Smith?' cried Mr Elton. 'I never thought of her in any way but as your friend. Oh! Who can think of Miss Smith when Miss Woodhouse is near!'

Emma was too overcome to speak. Mr Elton took the opportunity to seize her hand again.

'Charming Miss Woodhouse! Your silence suggests that you have long suspected how I feel. And dare I suggest—'

This was too much. Emma pulled her hand away.

'No, sir!' she cried. 'You may suggest nothing! Am I to understand that you have never thought seriously of my friend?'

Now it was Mr Elton's turn to be offended.

'*I* think seriously of Miss Smith?' he cried. 'Never! She is a good sort of girl and no doubt there are some men who might not object to ... but I?'

He paused, disgusted by the very idea. 'No, madam. My visits to Hartfield have been for yourself alone. And I must say, the encouragement I received—'

'Encouragement! *I* give you encouragement? Sir, you have been mistaken. I saw you as the admirer of my friend – nothing more. And,' Emma added firmly, 'I have no thoughts of marriage at present.'

Mr Elton was too angry to say another word and the rest of the journey passed in furious silence. Emma could not remember a time when she had been so miserable.

Poor Harriet. How could Emma have persuaded her into liking that man? How could she have been so wrong! How could Mr Knightley have been so right?

Part 2
Chapter 1
Miss Bates

Christmas was over and Mr Elton was gone. Emma's father had received a letter to say that he was leaving Highbury for several weeks to stay with friends in Bath. Emma was relieved. There would be no awkward encounters in the village, no embarrassing meetings at church. Not for a while, anyway.

But there was still Harriet. Emma felt ashamed. She knew the whole wretched business was her fault.

'It was I,' she said to herself, 'who actually talked Harriet into being attached to this man. She might never have thought of him but for me.'

She did not regret her part in persuading Harriet to refuse Mr Martin. No, there she was quite right. But there she should have stopped. She had been wrong to encourage her friend to think kindly of Mr Elton and resolved to give up matchmaking for good.

But first, poor Harriet must be told.

There were tears, of course there were. But, in general, Harriet took the news surprisingly well. The sweet girl had such a low opinion of herself that she was convinced she would never have deserved the affections of a man like Mr Elton anyway. Nobody but her dear friend

Miss Woodhouse would have thought it possible!

Harriet's tears made Emma ashamed all over again and even more determined to make amends. She would not leave Harriet's side for one moment, she decided. She would use her time to devise all sorts of interesting amusements and diverting pastimes to help her friend forget all about the gentleman.

But before that, they must call on Miss Bates.

'Oh! Miss Woodhouse! It is so kind of you to call, so very kind indeed. And Miss Smith too!' Miss Bates was a great talker, full of friendly chat and snippets of local news. 'I say, Mamma,' she continued, turning to the old lady who was seated with her knitting by the fire. 'Do you see who has come to call on us?'

There was no reply, so Miss Bates turned back to Emma.

'My mother is a little deaf, you know,' she said. 'But only a very little. If I raise my voice and say everything two or three times over, she is sure to hear. Am I not right, Mamma?'

There was still no reply, so Miss Bates continued, 'It is very remarkable that my mother always seems to hear Jane better than me, do you not agree, Miss Woodhouse? Dear Jane speaks so clearly!'

'Dear Jane' was Jane Fairfax, Miss Bates's niece. She often came to stay with her grandmother and aunt in

Highbury and was a great favourite with everyone in the
village. Except Emma.

'Are you expecting Miss Fairfax here again soon?'
said Emma.

'Oh! Yes, Miss Woodhouse! She is coming next week.
We are so pleased, so very pleased indeed – for she is to
be with us for three months. Is it not the most
delightful news?'

Emma had been hoping for Frank Churchill. Instead
she was to get Jane Fairfax.

For three months.

Chapter 2
Jane Fairfax

Jane Fairfax was an accomplished young woman; there was no doubt about that. And she was more than pretty – she was beautiful. Her eyes were a deep grey, with dark eyelashes and eyebrows; her figure was graceful; her manners were charming; her handwriting lovely; and her piano-playing exquisite.

Emma could not think why she did not like her.

Jane was reserved, it was true. While others talked, she sat quietly, wrapped up in a cloak of her own politeness. There was no getting at her real opinion, no knowing what she really thought. And then there was her aunt. Miss Bates always made such a great fuss of her: 'Jane is so very great a favourite!'; 'Jane is always so considerate!'; and, at the least little sniffle: 'Poor Jane has a cold! But she is so brave! She never complains!'

Jane, Jane, Jane. Before she had even arrived in Highbury, Emma was tired of hearing her name.

And now she was here. She had come, along with her aunt and grandmother, for a musical evening at Hartfield. Emma was first at the piano. She played well, everyone said so. Then Jane played and she played better. Nobody said so, but Emma knew it. And she suspected that Jane knew it too.

Miss Bates was talking: 'Oh! Dear Miss Woodhouse, you play so beautifully! Of course you have a fine instrument here at Hartfield on which to practise! Dear Jane has nothing at our poor little home. And yet she has such talent! 'Tis a shame, is it not, Mamma?' Her mother was sitting quietly by the fire as usual. 'I say, Mamma – '

The evening was going very slowly for poor Emma.

And then a new subject came up: Frank Churchill.

It transpired that he and Jane had been staying at Weymouth at the same time and had been seen together on several occasions. At last! Emma had an opportunity to discover something about the mysterious young man.

'How did you find Mr Churchill, Miss Fairfax?' she asked. 'Was he handsome?'

Jane believed he was thought to be a fine young man.

'Agreeable?'

Jane had heard he was generally thought so.

'Did he strike you as clever? Interesting? Amusing?'

Jane believed everybody found Mr Churchill's manner pleasing. It seemed that she had no opinion on the gentleman at all. And for that, Emma could not forgive her.

Chapter 3
News!

It was the following morning and Mr Knightley had called at Hartfield.

'I know you like news, Emma,' he said. 'And I heard something on my way here that I think will interest you.'

'Oh, yes, I always like news! What is it?'

Before Mr Knightley could reply, the door was thrown open, revealing Miss Bates and Miss Fairfax.

'Oh! My dear sir, my dear Miss Woodhouse! Have you heard the news?'

Mr Knightley had lost his moment. Miss Bates looked from one face to another and: 'Mr Elton is to be married!'

Emma was so completely surprised that she could not speak.

'That was my news,' said Mr Knightley, casting a quick look in her direction. 'I thought it would interest you, Emma.'

'It is a Miss Hawkins!' Miss Bates added quickly. 'A Miss Hawkins of Bath!'

Emma felt it was time she said something.

'Well!' she said. 'I'm sure Mr Elton and Miss Hawkins have everybody's wishes for their happiness.'

'Dear Miss Woodhouse! Always so thoughtful!

So concerned for others!'

'Still, one feels it cannot be a very long acquaintance,' Emma continued. 'Mr Elton has only been gone four weeks.'

Mr Knightley hid a smile.

'Yes! Only four weeks, as you observe, Miss Woodhouse!' cried Miss Bates. 'Oh! My mother is so pleased! Did she not say so, Jane? She said … '

Jane allowed her aunt to chat on uninterrupted for several more minutes until she remembered another appointment in the village.

'Well, I believe we must be running away! Oh! Mr Knightley is coming too. Well, that is so very – good morning to you, Miss Woodhouse! Mr Elton and Miss Hawkins! Of Bath!'

Emma was not alone five minutes to consider the news, when the door was flung open again.

'Oh! Miss Woodhouse! What do you think has happened?'

It was Harriet. She had clearly heard the news concerning Mr Elton's marriage. Emma felt the kindest thing she could do was listen quietly and wait for the tears to come.

But Harriet's news was of a very different kind. She had been in Ford's (the biggest and most important shop in the village) when who should come in?

Miss Woodhouse could not think.

'Elizabeth Martin, Miss Woodhouse – and her brother!'

Mr Martin. It was the first time Harriet had seen him since she turned down his proposal of marriage.

'I thought I should have fainted! I did not know what to do! And, Miss Woodhouse, what do you think?'

Again, Miss Woodhouse was at a loss.

'I was sure they were talking of me and I could not help thinking he was persuading her to speak to me – and indeed, she presently came forward and asked me how I did and seemed ready to shake hands! And then I found he was coming up towards me too – slowly, as if he did not quite know what to do – and he spoke, and I answered, and we stood for a minute, and then they left and – Oh! Miss Woodhouse! Do talk to me and make me comfortable again!'

It seemed that the news of Mr Elton's forthcoming marriage might not be so disturbing for Harriet after all.

Chapter 4
Mr Elton's Return

Mr Elton had left Highbury humbled and humiliated, rejected by one young lady; he came back smug, self-satisfied and engaged to another!

And not just any other. It was said in the village that the delightful Miss Hawkins (of Bath) was not just charming and well dressed; she was also in possession of a large fortune. It was no wonder that Mr Elton was walking around Highbury looking so very pleased with himself.

The wedding was to happen without delay and it was expected that the lady herself would soon be seen in the village, as Miss Hawkins no longer, but as Mrs Elton.

Emma had other things on her mind. She had been out walking with Harriet in the village when they met Mr and Mrs Weston. Emma was so glad to see her old friend that she did not at first hear what Mr Weston was saying: 'Yes! I had a letter this morning; it is a certainty, an absolute certainty. Frank comes tomorrow. We shall see him by dinner time, he says, and he comes for a whole fortnight.'

This was news indeed. Emma looked at her friend. Mrs Weston had not met Frank before and Emma knew she would be anxious about creating the right impression.

'Think of me tomorrow, dear Emma,' she said. 'About

four o'clock.'

'Four o'clock?' cried Mr Weston as they moved away to their carriage. 'Depend upon it, he will be here by three!'

The morning of the interesting day arrived and Emma did not forget her promise. She did not forget at nine, ten or eleven o'clock that she was to think of Mrs Weston at four.

The clock struck twelve as she passed through the hall.

Twelve o'clock, thought Emma. *I shall not forget to think of her in four hours' time. And by this time tomorrow, perhaps, I may be thinking of the possibility of them all calling here.*

She opened the parlour door. Two gentlemen were sitting with her father: Mr Weston ... and his son.

Frank Churchill had arrived.

Chapter 5
Frank Churchill

He was in front of her. The Frank Churchill so long talked about, the object of so much interest, was there, standing in her drawing room. He had reached the Westons' house the evening before and his father had wasted no time in bringing him over to meet Emma and her father.

'I told you!' cried Mr Weston. 'Did I not, Emma? I told you that he would be here earlier than he said!'

Emma could not think too much had been said in the young man's praise. He had a great deal of his father's spirit and liveliness and there was a well-bred ease of manner and a readiness to talk which convinced her that he was eager to be friends. And he was a very good-looking young man. Emma knew immediately that she would like him.

Introductions were made, pleasantries exchanged and, while the two fathers were chatting together (Mr Woodhouse was concerned that young Mr Churchill may have caught a cold on his journey), Frank took the opportunity to speak of his father's new wife.

'My father's marriage,' he said, speaking in a low voice so the gentleman in question should not hear, 'is the very wisest and best thing he could ever have done. Everyone must rejoice in it.'

Emma smiled. If Frank had not spoken kindly of her friend, she could not have continued to like him.

'We are all very pleased,' she said, 'to see Mr and Mrs Weston so happily settled.'

'It is more than a pleasure for me,' said Frank, 'to see my

father with such a wife at his side and such friends around him.'

He was very much pleased with everything, it seemed: his father's marriage, his father's house, the walk to Highbury, the village itself – he had seen several pretty houses on the way over, though none as fine as the one in which he found himself at present …

And Emma? She could not help but wonder if Mr Frank Churchill was as pleased with her as he appeared to be with everything else. Was that what she wanted? She could not be sure.

But he was a very good-looking young man.

The visit was over too quickly. Mr Weston had business in the village, he said, but – this with a quick look in Frank's direction – he need not hurry anyone else.

His son was too polite to ignore the hint.

'As you are going on business, sir,' he said, getting to his feet, 'I will take the opportunity of paying a brief visit.'

'A visit, Frank? A visit to whom? I was not aware you had friends in the area.'

Frank turned to Emma. 'I have the honour of being acquainted with a neighbour of yours,' he said. 'A lady, who is staying in or near Highbury I believe.'

A lady – ?

Frank looked at Emma with his easy smile. 'She goes by the name of Fairfax,' he went on. 'A Miss Jane Fairfax.'

Chapter 6
The Party

It was a few days later, and Mr and Mrs Cole were having a party. Mr Woodhouse was not fond of late nights or large gatherings where everybody talked at once so Emma went in the carriage on her own, full of the agreeable prospect of spending an evening with Frank Churchill.

'I declare,' Mrs Cole was saying as Emma arrived, 'I do not know when I have heard anything that has given me more satisfaction!'

A present for Jane Fairfax had arrived at Miss Bates's house the day before. It was a brand-new piano, a most elegant-looking instrument, and nobody knew where it had come from!

Emma was interested. 'A fine present indeed,' she said. 'And Miss Fairfax has no idea as to who might have sent it?'

'No, Miss Woodhouse! That is the mystery of it! No one has any idea at all!'

Emma turned to Frank, who had just arrived and was listening to the conversation. 'What is your opinion, Mr Churchill? Why do you smile?'

'Me?' he said. 'I suppose I smile for pleasure at Miss Fairfax's good fortune. It is a handsome present.'

'My dear Emma,' Mrs Weston had appeared. 'I am longing to talk to you.' She drew her friend aside. 'I have made a discovery! Do you know how Miss Bates and her niece came here tonight?'

'They walked, I imagine.'

'No, Emma. They came in a carriage ... Mr Knightley's carriage!'

'That was kind of him.'

'You do not think there was more to it than kindness?'

'My dear Mrs Weston, what can you mean?'

'A suspicion has darted into my head, Emma, and I have not been able to get it out again. The more I think of it, the more likely it appears.'

'You do not suggest – '

'Yes! I have made a match between Mr Knightley and Jane Fairfax!'

'Mr Knightley and Jane Fairfax? Dear Mrs Weston, how could you think such a thing? Mr Knightley must not marry! It is quite impossible!'

'She has always been a favourite with him, Emma, you know that. And this piano – may it not be from Mr Knightley? He is just the person to do it!'

'You take up an idea, Mrs Weston, and run away with it. Nothing will ever convince me that Mr Knightley has any thought of marrying Jane Fairfax. Or anybody else!'

Emma found the very idea absurd. But she also found it quite difficult to enjoy the rest of the evening. Even when Frank Churchill asked her to dance.

Chapter 7
The Piano

It was the day after the party and Emma had sat down at her own piano to do an hour's vigorous practice when her good intentions were cut short by the arrival of a breathless Harriet.

'Oh, Miss Woodhouse!' she said. 'What do you think? Anne Cox told me something just now – you know her, Miss Woodhouse, she is a tall girl with a long, yellow face, you've often remarked upon it when we've passed her in the lane – Anne Cox told me that Mr Martin dined with them last Saturday!'

It seemed that Harriet had quite recovered from her disappointment over Mr Elton's marriage.

'She said he sat by her at dinner and was most agreeable! What do you think, Miss Woodhouse? I think she likes him! What shall I do?'

Miss Woodhouse thought it was time for a walk. Her piano practice would have to wait.

As they were making their way to Ford's (they had some pretty new muslins that Emma hoped would take Harriet's mind off Mr Martin), they met Mrs Weston and Miss Bates coming out of the door laden with packages.

'My dear Miss Woodhouse!' cried Miss Bates. 'I am so

glad! And Miss Smith! How do you do?'

'Very well, thank you, Miss Bates,' said Emma. 'I hope Mrs Bates—'

'Oh, thank you, Miss Woodhouse, thank you, delightfully well. I said to my mother – it would be such an honour if dear Miss Woodhouse were to call and give us her opinion on Jane's fine new instrument!'

'Do come, Emma,' said Mrs Weston. 'I have left Frank at Miss Bates's house just now.'

'He is mending my mother's spectacles!' said Miss Bates. 'So obliging, so very obliging, such a very obliging young man! The rivet came out, you know, and Jane said – '

Emma said she and Harriet would be pleased to call at Miss Bates's. And so the little party moved off down the street.

The appearance of the little sitting room was tranquility itself. Mrs Bates was dozing by the fire; Frank was at the table, busy with her spectacles; and Jane was standing with her back to them, intent on her pianoforte.

Frank looked up as they entered. 'You find me trying to be useful, Miss Woodhouse,' he said with a smile. 'Tell me if you think I shall succeed.'

'Have you not finished, Frank?' said Mrs Weston. 'You would not make a very good living as a spectacle-mender at this rate!'

'I have been assisting Miss Fairfax in trying to make her instrument stand steady,' said Frank. 'An unevenness in the floor, I believe. You see, we have been wedging one leg with paper. Miss Fairfax?'

Jane turned, startled at the sound of her name.

'Will you give your friends the pleasure of hearing you play?'

Jane blushed and looked away.

'And if you are feeling very kind,' Frank continued, with a sly look at Emma, 'you will play one of those waltz tunes we danced to last night. Let me live them over again!'

And so Jane played. Emma joined everyone in their praise of her skill and talent and resolved to finish her own practice as soon as she got home.

'What a pleasure it is,' said Frank, 'to hear a tune again that has made you happy. Do you not agree, Miss Woodhouse? That last one you played, Miss Fairfax. If I am not mistaken, it was one you and I danced to when we were at Weymouth.'

Jane looked up at him and blushed deeply. Frank held her gaze for a moment before going back to his work on Mrs Bates's spectacles with a small smile.

'It is done!' he said, turning to the old lady with a bow. 'I have the pleasure, madam, of restoring your spectacles.'

As he was being thanked by both mother and daughter,

Miss Bates caught sight of someone passing by outside the window.

'Mr Knightley! Mr Knightley, I declare!' She opened the window and leaned out. 'Pray come in, do come in! You will find some friends here!'

'How is your niece, Miss Bates?' they heard Mr Knightley reply. 'I hope she caught no cold last night?'

From across the room, Mrs Weston gave Emma a look of particular meaning. Emma looked away.

'Do come in, Mr Knightley! Who do you think is here? Miss Woodhouse! And Mrs Weston! Mr Churchill is here too! He has mended my mother's spectacles.'

'No,' said Mr Knightley. 'Thank you, Miss Bates. It sounds as if your room is full enough already. I will call to hear Miss Fairfax play when you have fewer visitors.'

And with that he was gone, leaving Emma to wonder: *Why was it that Mr Knightley preferred to see Jane Fairfax without other visitors? Could it be that Mrs Weston was right? Was it Mr Knightley who had sent the piano?*

Was it possible that he did have feelings for her?

And why should that trouble Emma quite so much?

Chapter 8
Frank's Goodbye

Since he arrived in Highbury, Emma had seen Frank nearly every day and could not help but notice the looks that were exchanged between Mr and Mrs Weston whenever they were together. They were glad the two young people were friends, it was clear, and perhaps hoped that they might become more than that. Emma was not sure. She liked Frank; he was lively and charming and amusing. She knew they made a fine couple. But was she in love? She was not sure.

And there was to be no time to find out.

A letter had arrived from Frank's adopted family. His aunt was ill. He must go to her at once.

'Of all the horrid things, leave-taking is the worst,' Frank was saying. He had called at Hartfield to say goodbye. Emma had never seen him so quiet, so sorrowful, so dejected.

'But you will come again,' she said. 'This will not be your only visit to Highbury?'

Frank shook his head. 'Ah!' he said. 'I shall try! But, my aunt –'

Emma had heard about Frank's aunt; she was very rich, very demanding and very often ill.

'And you must be off this very morning?'

'Yes. My father is to join me here any moment. We shall walk back together and then I must leave at once.'

Emma smiled. 'You cannot spare five minutes for your friends Miss Fairfax and Miss Bates?' she said, trying to lift his spirits. 'How unlucky! A call on Miss Bates is usually enough to make anyone glad to leave Highbury!'

'What? Oh! I have been there already,' Frank replied. 'I was passing their door and thought it the right thing to do ... '

He hesitated, got up, walked to the window, turned.

'Miss Woodhouse,' he said, 'I think you can hardly be quite without suspicion ... '

He stopped, looking at her as if wanting to read her thoughts. Emma forced herself to speak calmly.

'You were quite right, Mr Churchill,' she said. 'It was kind of you to call on Miss Bates.'

Frank was silent. She knew he was looking at her. A few awkward moments passed. Then he tried again: 'Miss Woodhouse, forgive me – there is something I must ... '

Who could say how it might have ended if his father had not arrived at that moment? Emma did not know if she was pleased or sorry when Mr Weston entered the room, followed by her own father. It was time for Frank to go.

A friendly shake of the hand, an earnest 'Goodbye' and that was it.

Frank Churchill was gone.

Chapter 9
Mrs Elton

Highbury seemed a dull place without Frank Churchill. Emma missed his attentions, his liveliness, his manners – and he had almost told her that he loved her ...

She amused herself by imagining various letters he might send, conversations they might have, dances they might attend together. And it struck her that every imaginary scene between them ended in the same way: Frank proposed marriage and Emma refused him.

Perhaps she was not in love at all.

Meanwhile, more news was flying round the village: Mr Elton's marriage had taken place; he would soon be back in Highbury – with his new wife.

Emma was as curious as anyone to see what kind of woman she might be.

She did not have to wait long. Mr Elton and his bride were soon established in the vicarage and everyone – including Miss Woodhouse, of course – was expected to call on them. It would be the first time Emma had seen Mr Elton since their encounter in the carriage and she expected the visit to be somewhat awkward and embarrassing. So she decided to take Harriet.

The call was made. Mr Elton did not appear and Mrs Elton talked of nothing but herself and the wealthy friends and family she had left behind in Bath. Emma took Harriet away as soon as she could without appearing ill-mannered.

'Well, Miss Woodhouse,' said Harriet as they were walking back to Hartfield. 'What do you think? Is she not charming? And so well dressed! It is really no surprise that Mr Elton fell in love.'

'Indeed,' Emma replied. 'She was an unmarried woman with a very large fortune and he happened to meet her. It is no surprise at all.'

A few days later, and their visit was returned. Mrs Elton came to Hartfield.

'What a charming house, Miss Woodhouse!' cried the lady as she walked in the door. 'It quite reminds me of my brother-in-law's estate at Maple Grove! Did I tell you about my sister's husband? Mr Suckling of the Bristol Sucklings? Quite a well-respected family in the county – I am surprised you have not heard of them.'

She looked around.

'Oh! I am quite struck by the likeness of your sweet house to theirs! It is not so large, of course, and the grounds are not so extensive, but it is all so neat and pretty! Quite perfect for the two of you, just yourself and your dear father!'

Emma was about to reply but Mrs Elton was speaking again. 'And where do you think we have just come from? The Westons! Oh! He is quite a favourite with me already! And she appears truly good, such a motherly creature!' Here, Mrs Elton paused and gave a discreet cough before continuing: 'She was your – ahem – governess, I think?'

Emma nodded. 'For sixteen years. And she is now my dearest friend.'

'Yes, I had heard as much! And knowing it, I must say I was quite astonished to find her so ladylike! She is really quite the gentlewoman!'

Emma was unable to speak. Astonished that the person who brought her up should be a gentlewoman! There was more.

'And who do you think called when we were there?' Mrs Elton continued. 'Knightley!'

Knightley?

'Was that not lucky? He is such a particular friend of Mr E. I had a great curiosity to meet him. And I am pleased to say that my lord and master' (this with an affected little laugh) 'need not be ashamed of his friend!'

Lord and master?

'Oh yes, Miss Woodhouse! I tell you, Knightley is quite the gentleman!'

Happily, Mrs Elton soon decided that her lord and master would be wondering where she was. She went, and Emma could breathe.

Insufferable woman, she thought, *with her 'Mr E' and her 'lord and master' and her 'Knightley'!* She was more unbearable than Emma could ever have imagined.

But Emma's thoughts were interrupted by the arrival of Mrs Weston brandishing a letter.

Frank Churchill was coming back.

And Emma had not the least idea how she felt about it.

Part 3
Chapter 1
The Ball

Mr and Mrs Weston had decided to celebrate Frank's return in style. There was to be a ball, a proper one, with music and dancing, held in rooms at the Crown, the largest and most important inn in the village. It would be the event of the year!

The day approached, the day arrived; and Frank was restless. He was standing with Emma, alongside his father and Mrs Weston, waiting to greet the guests. But he could not keep still. He was looking about, going to the door, listening for the arrival of the carriages. Was it just that he was impatient for the dancing to begin? Or was there something else on his mind?

Mr and Mrs Elton were the first to arrive. Frank moved away to greet some more arrivals, leaving Mrs Elton to give Mr Weston her opinion of his son.

'A very fine young man, Mr Weston,' she said. 'I am happy to say that I am extremely pleased with him. His manners are precisely what I like – truly the gentleman without the least conceit or snobbism. You must know I have a vast dislike of snobs – they were never tolerated at Maple Grove.'

Before Mr Weston could respond, another voice was heard: 'So very obliging of you! No rain at all! I do not care for myself – quite thick shoes! Oh! Look at this room!'

Miss Bates had arrived.

'This is brilliant indeed! Such a noble fire! Mrs Weston, I must say – do you like Jane's hair? She did it all herself! Oh! Mr Frank Churchill, I must tell you my mother's spectacles have never been at fault since … ! My mother often talks of you. Does she not, Jane? Do we not often talk of Mr Frank Churchill?'

Jane smiled and blushed, but Miss Bates did not wait for a reply.

'Ah, here's Miss Woodhouse! And Miss Smith! Oh this is delightful! So many old friends! How do you do?'

Frank had returned to his place beside Emma.

'How do you like Mrs Elton?' she said in a whisper.

'Not at all,' he replied. 'When are we going to begin dancing?'

He looked over to where Jane was standing next to her aunt and raised his voice slightly. 'You are promised to me, Miss Woodhouse, remember?' he said. 'I will dance with no one else tonight!'

And so they danced. Emma was happy. She and Frank were well-matched as partners and she knew that they were a couple worth looking at. She noticed more smiling looks passing between Mr and Mrs Weston as they watched, and wondered again whether she was in love.

Jane Fairfax did not dance. And neither, Emma saw, did Mr Knightley. She could not approve of this. He was standing with a group of older men, the husbands and the fathers, where he ought not to be – he ought to be dancing! His tall, upright figure appeared out of place among the bulky forms and stooping shoulders of the elderly men. Whenever she caught his eye, she tried to force him to smile. But he remained serious, watching her as she flew past with her partner.

Everyone else seemed happy. Except Jane Fairfax, of course, who was standing to the side with her aunt.

And Harriet.

Emma was suddenly aware that her friend had no partner. She was sitting on her own at the side of the room, looking very lonely and forlorn. *This could not be allowed,* thought Emma. *There must be some kind gentleman who would take pity on the poor girl.*

'Do you not dance, Mr Elton?' Mrs Weston had also noticed Harriet's plight.

'Most readily, Mrs Weston, if you will dance with me,' the gentleman replied with his smooth smile.

'Me? Oh no! I am no dancer,' she said. 'I will get you a better partner than myself. There is a young lady here who I would be glad to see dancing! Miss Smith?'

Harriet looked up at the mention of her name and smiled gratefully. But Mr Elton shook his head.

'Miss Smith? Oh!' He looked at his wife and suppressed a little smile. 'No, Mrs Weston, you must excuse me. I am an old married man. My dancing days are over.'

And with that, he turned his back on the ladies and went off with his wife, exchanging looks of great amusement. Harriet blushed deeply and Mrs Weston said no more. Emma felt her face quite hot with anger. *So this was Mr Elton! Kind, obliging Mr Elton, who thought it funny to humiliate her poor friend in front of everyone!*

And then she heard Mrs Elton: 'Oh, look! Knightley has taken pity on Miss Smith! Very good-natured of him, I'm sure!'

It was true. Mr Knightley was leading Harriet onto the dance floor and Mr Elton retreated into the other room, looking (Emma thought) very foolish. Emma longed to thank Mr Knightley: it was an act so typical of him – kind, gentlemanly, thoughtful. Now she could really enjoy herself!

Supper was announced, supper was served, everyone returned to the ballroom and Mr Weston was calling on everyone to begin dancing again: 'Come, Miss Woodhouse, Miss Cox, Miss Smith, what are you all doing? Emma! Set an example! Everybody is lazy! Everybody is asleep!'

Emma looked around for Frank. 'I am ready,' she said. 'Whenever I am wanted.'

'Whom are you going to dance with?' said a familiar voice.

Emma hesitated. 'With you, if you ask me.'

'Then I ask you. Will you?' He offered her his hand.

'Indeed I will.' She took his hand and Mr Knightley led her onto the dance floor.

Chapter 2
Harriet's Precious Treasures

It was the morning after the dance and Emma was thinking about Frank Churchill. She had seen him out of the corner of her eye while she was dancing with Mr Knightley. He was by the fire talking to Jane Fairfax, asking her something, trying to persuade her to dance, perhaps. Jane was shaking her head, refusing to meet his eye, and when Frank took her hand, she pulled it away and moved off to stand with her aunt. Frank watched her go and then turned and walked out of the room.

What could it mean?

Emma's thoughts were interrupted by the arrival of Harriet, who burst into the room with a small parcel in her hand.

'Miss Woodhouse! Excuse me, I have something I would like to tell you – if you have time?'

Emma assured her that she did.

'It is a sort of confession, Miss Woodhouse! And then, once you know everything, it will be over!'

Emma was intrigued. What could Harriet possibly have to confess?

'Something happened last night, Miss Woodhouse, that made me realize how foolish I have been.'

'With regard to – ?'

'Him.'

Ah. Of course. Him.

'I can see nothing in him now, nothing. Oh, and his wife!' Harriet gave a little shudder. 'Oh, she is very charming, I dare say, and well dressed and all that, but I think she is also extremely ill-tempered and disagreeable! I shall never forget her look last night.'

'Neither shall I,' said Emma. 'And I am very glad your eyes have been opened. Mr Elton is not the superior creature you – or I – believed him to be.'

'And that is why I have come. I am going to destroy something I should have destroyed long ago. Something I should never have kept.' Harriet blushed. 'Miss Woodhouse, can you guess what this parcel holds?'

Miss Woodhouse could not.

'Some things that I have valued very much.'

Harriet held the parcel towards her and Emma read the words 'MOST PRECIOUS TREASURES' on the top. Harriet unwrapped it. Inside, there was a pretty wooden box, lined with some sort of soft cotton material. Emma looked closer. Other than the material, she could see only a small piece of sticking plaster – the sort of thing you would use to cover up a little cut or graze.

'Now,' said Harriet. 'You must remember.'

'Indeed I do not.'

'It was in this very room – a few days before I had my sore throat. Mr Elton cut his finger with your new penknife and you said he needed a plaster? But, as you had none with you, and you knew I had, you asked me. So I took mine out of my bag and cut him a piece, but it was too large, so he cut it smaller and then he kept playing with what was left before he gave it back to me.'

'Oh, Harriet ... '

'So I, in my nonsense, could not help but make a treasure of it and put it in my special box and would take it out and look at it now and then as a treat!'

Emma was divided between wonder and amusement. *Would she ever want to keep a piece of plaster that Frank Churchill had been playing with?* She didn't think so.

'And here is something else,' Harriet continued. 'Something even more valuable.'

It was the end of an old pencil.

'This was really his,' she said. 'It really did belong to him. Do you not remember?'

Emma shook her head.

'Well! It was one morning, I forget what day exactly, he wanted to write something in his notebook, but when he took out his pencil, there was no lead left in it, so you lent him another, and this was left upon the table. I kept my eye on it and then, as soon as I dared, I picked it up and never parted with it again!'

Emma smiled. 'What else have you got in your box, Harriet?'

'That's all. And now I am going to throw them in the fire. There! That is the end, thank goodness, of Mr Elton!'

The two young ladies watched as Harriet's treasures flared up in the fireplace.

67

Harriet broke the silence, with a serious face.

'I shall never marry, Miss Woodhouse.'

'Because of Mr Elton?'

'Oh no! No!' Harriet blushed, looked down, mumbled something. Emma just caught the words: '… so superior to him … '

'Harriet, is there – someone else?'

'I would never presume that he could like me, Miss Woodhouse, he is far too … Oh! It is just a pleasure to admire him from a distance.'

'And your feelings for this gentleman began – ?'

'Last night, Miss Woodhouse. At the dance. He had such a noble look. So graceful, so charming. Such a dancer.'

So Harriet's heart was now set on Frank Churchill. Well, he was a very handsome young man.

Chapter 3
Box Hill

'Ladies and gentlemen! I have an order from Miss Woodhouse!'

Summer had arrived, and Mr Weston had organized an outing to Box Hill, a beauty spot a few miles from Highbury. Emma had never been there before and she wanted to see what everybody else found so well worth seeing.

The outing was not going well. The day was hot and nobody had much to say. Jane Fairfax was quiet and preoccupied; the Eltons walked around on their own, ignoring everybody else; and Mr Knightley stared thoughtfully at the view. Frank Churchill was trying to make amends for the dullness of the others by being especially talkative and merry.

'Ladies and gentlemen!' he repeated, 'I am ordered by Miss Woodhouse to say that she desires to know what you are all thinking of!'

Emma was the only one who laughed. 'Indeed, Mr Churchill,' she said, 'that is the very last thing I want! To know what everyone is thinking could cause all kinds of difficulties!'

'Very well,' Frank said in an undertone. 'I will try something else.' He turned back to the others. 'Ladies and gentlemen!' he announced again. 'I am ordered by Miss Woodhouse to say that she no longer desires to know exactly what you are thinking of, but only requires something very entertaining from each of you!'

There was a general rustle of discomfort. Only Miss Bates tried to enter the spirit of the game. 'Oh dear!' she cried. 'I am not sure that I will be able to think of anything very entertaining! I must leave that to others who have more wit! I think, perhaps, that Jane – '

'Miss Woodhouse demands from each of you either one thing very clever, two things moderately clever – or three things very dull indeed!'

'Then I need not be uneasy,' said Miss Bates. 'Three things very dull indeed! That will just do for me. I shall be sure to say three dull things just as soon as I open my mouth, shan't I?'

She looked around at everyone for their approval.

Emma could not resist. 'Ah, ma'am, but that might be difficult,' she said. 'For you are limited to only three dull things. Only three!'

Miss Bates did not immediately understand.

'Oh!' she said. And then, 'Oh … ' as she realized what Emma had meant. She blinked her eyes very fast and turned her head away to address Mr Knightley. 'I see what she means. I will try not to talk so much. Oh dear! I must make myself very disagreeable or she would not have said such a thing to an old friend.'

Mr Knightley looked at Emma. Emma looked away. Then Mrs Elton spoke up.

'Mr E and I are not at all fond of this sort of thing,' she declared. 'Please, Mr Churchill, you must excuse us from your clever games.'

'Indeed,' said her husband. 'I have nothing to say that can entertain Miss Woodhouse. Shall we walk, Augusta?'

They got up and stalked away.

'Happy couple!' said Frank as soon as they were out of hearing. 'How well they suit one another. Very lucky, marrying as they did after such a very short acquaintance.'

Jane Fairfax looked up. He met her eyes for a second before continuing: 'It was only a few weeks that they knew each other before they got married, I understand,' he said. 'I wonder how many a man has committed himself to a woman on such a short acquaintance and regretted it the rest of his life?'

'Such things may occur undoubtedly,' said Jane. 'An unfortunate attachment may arise between a man and a woman who have only known each other for a short time. But it is only weak people who allow such a thing to affect them forever.'

Frank bowed his head, and then changed the subject.

'Well! I have so little confidence in my own judgement that whenever I marry, I hope somebody will choose my wife for me.' Frank turned to Emma. 'Will you?'

Emma smiled. 'By all means.'

'I have two requests: she must be very lively and have hazel eyes! I ask for nothing else. I shall go abroad for a couple of years and when I return I shall come to you for my wife, Miss Woodhouse. Remember!'

Jane had got to her feet. 'Now, ma'am,' she said to her aunt. 'Shall we join Mrs Elton?'

They walked off. Mr Knightley followed them, leaving Emma with Mr Weston and his son. Frank's spirits rose to an almost unpleasant pitch, and even Emma began to feel tired of his flattery and jokes. Thankfully, it was soon time to go.

'Emma, I must speak to you.'

She was waiting for her carriage when she found Mr Knightley at her side.

'How could you be so unfeeling to Miss Bates?'

Emma blushed and tried to laugh it off.

'Oh, it was not so very bad. I dare say she did not understand what I said.'

'I assure you she did, Emma. She has talked of it since, and I wish you could have heard the excuses she made for your unkindness.'

'Oh!'

'It was badly done, Emma. You, whom she has known since you were a baby, to laugh at her, humble her, in front of her niece. In front of everyone!'

Emma could not speak. She knew he was right.

'This is not pleasant to you Emma and it is far from pleasant to me, but I cannot see you acting wrongly without saying anything. I must, I *will* tell you the truth when I can.'

The carriage had arrived. She stepped inside, still unable to say anything, but then, not wanting Mr Knightley to think worse of her than he did already, leaned out to say goodbye. It was too late. He had turned away and the horses started to move.

Emma sank back in her seat as the carriage moved away and felt the tears running down her cheeks. *How could she have been so cruel to poor Miss Bates? And how could she let Mr Knightley think so badly of her?*

The tears continued to flow and did not stop until the carriage arrived at Hartfield.

Chapter 4
The Next Day

'I am afraid Miss Fairfax is not very well.' It was the morning after the disastrous outing to Box Hill and Emma had called at the Bates's, hoping to make amends for her rudeness the day before. She arrived to find the little house in a flurry. The maid had looked awkward and frightened when she opened the door, and as she walked in, Emma caught a glimpse of Jane Fairfax in the next room, looking very white-faced and ill, and heard Miss Bates's anxious fluttering voice: 'Well, my dear, I shall say you are laid down on the bed. I am sure you are ill enough.'

The next moment, Miss Bates came bustling through. She was talking just as much as usual but Emma could see she had been crying.

'Oh, Miss Woodhouse, what a pleasure, so very kind. Miss Smith? Ah, no, I see you are on your own. I am afraid you will have to excuse dear Jane, she has a dreadful headache.'

She paused to brush away a tear.

'I suppose you have heard the news, Miss Woodhouse, and have come to give us joy. Though it does not feel like joy to me. It will be hard for us to part with her, very hard.'

Emma was puzzled. 'Am I to understand that Miss Fairfax … '

'Has secured a situation, Miss Woodhouse – a fine opportunity, but a great change for my mother and me, a very great change.'

Emma knew that Jane Fairfax had no money of her own and could not depend on her aunt and grandmother to support her forever; if she did not marry she would need to find employment as a governess.

'She has been thinking of it for some time and now this situation has arisen, and so she has decided – ' Miss Bates stopped and blew her nose.

'And where, may I ask?'

'To a Mrs Smallridge, Miss Woodhouse. Charming woman, three little girls, delightful children. And only four miles from Maple Grove.'

Maple Grove?

'That is the home of Mrs Elton's sister and her husband, is it not?' said Emma.

'Yes, it was she who heard of the situation and entreated Jane to accept. Jane was against the idea at first, but changed her mind quite suddenly last evening when we returned from Box Hill. It was just after we heard that Mr Churchill had gone, I remember. My mother was looking for her spectacles.'

This was too much news for one day. Emma could

not take it in.

'Mr Churchill has left us again?'

'Oh yes, last night, in a great hurry. He had to go to his aunt. Not even time to say goodbye.' She brushed away another tear. 'Mrs Smallridge! A most elegant woman! And the children! Jane will be treated with such kindness!'

'And when is Miss Fairfax to leave you?'

'Very soon, very soon indeed; within a fortnight. My poor mother does not know how to bear it.'

So Jane Fairfax was to leave Highbury to begin life as a governess. And Frank Churchill had left without a word, summoned once again to the bedside of his wealthy aunt. As Emma walked back to Hartfield she thought about the fate of the two women. *One had money, so could summon her nephew whenever the fancy took her. The other had nothing. Just her brains and her beauty, and an aunt and grandmother who loved her and whom she had to leave. It did not seem fair – it was not fair!*

Emma wished that she had been a better friend to Jane Fairfax.

Chapter 5
Mrs Weston's News

For the whole of the last week, Highbury had been buzzing with the news: Frank's aunt, the wealthy Mrs Churchill who was so very often ill and so very often recovered, had actually died! It seemed that her last illness had been perfectly genuine: she had lived only a few hours after her nephew's arrival. Everyone felt suitably sad and the woman who had been so heartily disliked was now spoken of with kindness and respect.

But this was not the reason that Mr Weston appeared at Hartfield that morning with an urgent summons from his wife. Emma was alarmed.

'Is Mrs Weston unwell?'

'No, no, just a little agitated. She would have ordered the carriage and come to you, but she must see you alone. Can you come?'

Emma could. They set off together without delay.

'I have brought her, my dear,' Mr Weston said as they arrived. 'And I shall leave you together.'

Mrs Weston was looking so upset that Emma's uneasiness increased.

'What is it, my dear friend?' she said, sitting down and taking her hand. 'Tell me what has happened.'

'Have you really no idea, Emma?'

'None.'

Mrs Weston took a deep breath. 'It is Frank,' she said.

'Is Mr Churchill unwell? I know his aunt has died, but – '

'No, no, it is not that. He has been here this morning.' Mrs Weston hesitated. 'He came to speak to his father, Emma. To announce ... an attachment.'

'An attachment?' Emma thought first of herself, and then of Harriet.

'More than an attachment. An engagement. An actual engagement.'

'An *engagement*?'

'Frank Churchill is engaged, Emma – has long been engaged – to Miss Fairfax.'

Emma actually jumped with surprise. 'Jane Fairfax! You are not serious!'

'There has been a solemn engagement between them ever since they met in Weymouth.'

'But that was before either of them came to Highbury!'

Mrs Weston nodded.

'And they kept it a secret from everybody?' Emma felt her face grow hot with anger. 'Abominable! To come amongst us, pretending to be mere acquaintances! It is beyond low, Mrs Weston!'

'They had no choice, Emma. Jane has no money of her own. Frank's aunt would never have approved the match.'

'But now the lady has died … ?'

Mrs Weston nodded. 'His uncle has been told and gave his consent with very little persuasion.'

There was a pause. Mrs Weston reached out and touched Emma's hand.

'But … my Emma … there is one part of Frank's behaviour we cannot excuse.'

'His attentions to me?'

Mrs Weston nodded.

'My dearest Mrs Weston, please do not be concerned,' said Emma. 'There was a time that I did like him and even thought I might become attached. But it was only a short time. For the last few weeks I have viewed Mr Churchill as no more than an amusing acquaintance and the son of my dearest friend.'

Mrs Weston hugged her. 'Oh, Emma, I am so relieved! It was this that was worrying us most – that you might have been hurt by his behaviour.'

'Believe me, Mrs Weston, I care nothing for him. But this does not excuse him. What right did he have to pay me such attentions when he was engaged to another? And Jane? How could she bear it?'

And Harriet?

If, as Emma suspected, she had transferred her affections from Mr Elton to Frank Churchill, how would she take the news that he was engaged to someone else?

Chapter 6
Harriet and the News

Harriet called round the next day. Emma's heart beat fast as she heard her footsteps approaching. Poor Harriet! To be so disappointed again!

'Well, Miss Woodhouse!' she cried, coming eagerly into the room. 'Is not this the oddest news that ever was?'

Emma was puzzled. 'What news do you mean?'

'About Jane Fairfax. Mr Weston has just told me. He said it was a great secret and that I wasn't to mention it to anybody but you, as you already knew it.'

This was most peculiar. 'What did Mr Weston tell you?' Emma said.

'That Jane Fairfax and Mr Frank Churchill have been secretly engaged all this while. Did you ever hear anything so strange? I suppose it was he who sent the piano.'

Harriet showed no agitation, disappointment or even concern over the discovery. Emma looked at her, quite unable to speak.

'Had you any idea,' continued Harriet, 'of his being in love with her?'

'Not the slightest suspicion,' replied Emma. 'And you may be sure that if I had, Harriet, I would have warned you.'

'Me?' cried Harriet. 'Why would you warn me?'

Then, as she realized: 'Miss Woodhouse! You do not think I care for Mr Frank Churchill?'

'You cannot deny,' said Emma, 'that you gave me reason to think you did.'

Harriet pulled a face. 'Him? No! Never, never, never! I hope I have better taste than to think that way of Mr Frank Churchill! Dear Miss Woodhouse, how could you so misunderstand me?'

'Misunderstand you?' Emma looked at her. 'Harriet, are you telling me that you do not care for Frank Churchill – but you do care for someone else?'

Harriet nodded and sighed. 'A man so far superior that Frank Churchill is nobody at his side.'

Emma did not want to listen to the suspicion that was growing in her mind.

'Harriet,' she said quietly, 'There can be no more misunderstanding between us. The man you are speaking of, to whom you have become attached, is it – Mr Knightley?'

'I thought you knew! Ever since he came up and asked me to dance, Miss Woodhouse, when Mr Elton ignored me and there was no other partner in the room – that was when I began to feel how superior he was to every other being on earth.'

Emma took a deep breath. She did not understand why her heart was beating so fast.

'And have you any idea, Harriet, of Mr Knightley – returning your affection?'

Harriet blushed prettily and looked at her hands. 'Yes,' she replied quietly, looking up into Emma's face. 'Yes, Miss Woodhouse, I do believe that I have.'

Chapter 7
Mr Knightley

It was the next morning. Emma had felt too troubled to sit indoors and was walking in the garden, asking herself some questions.

Why was it so much worse that Harriet was in love with Mr Knightley than with Frank Churchill? And why was the evil so dreadfully increased by Harriet having some hope that her affections were returned? Emma knew the answer, of course she did. In a way she'd always known it: *Mr Knightley must marry no one but herself!*

It was only now, when she thought she might lose him, that she realized how much her happiness had always depended upon him. His visits, their walks together, even their quarrels, had meant more to her than a thousand dances with Frank Churchill. *But was Harriet right? Could it be true that Mr Knightley had begun to care for her?* Emma stared at the pleasant scene in front of her. The sun was shining, the air was soft and clear and smelled of wet grass and flowers. Everything was lovely. And Emma could not bear it.

'Emma?'

She turned and saw him, passing through the garden door and walking towards her.

'Mr Knightley!'

The 'how do you do's were quiet and restrained on each side. Emma thought he neither looked nor spoke cheerfully and wondered if, like her, he had something on his mind.

They walked together. He was silent; so silent that Emma was afraid. Perhaps he had come to tell her of his attachment to Harriet. She did not think she could bear it. Yet neither could she bear this silence.

'You have some news to hear,' she said, trying to smile, 'that I think will rather surprise you.'

'Have I?' he said quietly, turning to look at her. 'Of what nature?'

'Oh! The best nature in the world – a wedding!'

'If you mean Miss Fairfax and Frank Churchill, I have

heard that already. Mr Weston told me this morning. I came here straight away.'

'You are not surprised?'

'No. I long suspected there was something between them.'

'Indeed? Then you are more observant than I am. I never had the least idea.'

Mr Knightley seemed to be struggling with feelings she did not recognize.

'Abominable scoundrel,' he said in a low voice. 'To behave as he did, to you, when all the time ... '

He controlled himself and said in a louder steadier voice: 'I blame myself, Emma. I should have told you my suspicions.'

Emma found her arm drawn within his and pressed against his heart.

'Time, my dearest Emma, will heal the wound. He will soon be gone. And you will forget him.'

So that was it. Emma took a deep breath.

'You are very kind, Mr Knightley, but you are mistaken,' she said. 'I have no reason to regret Mr Churchill's engagement to another woman.'

He stopped. He turned to look at her. 'No reason?'

'No reason at all.'

'But I thought, when I saw you together, your behaviour – '

'I have very little to say for my conduct, Mr Knightley,' said Emma. 'Mr Churchill is the son of my friend, I was flattered by his attentions and allowed myself to appear pleased by them. That is all.'

'Oh, Emma!' He frowned as another thought struck him. 'I am sorry for her, though. Jane Fairfax deserves a better fate.'

'I have no doubt of their being happy together,' said Emma. 'Mrs Weston believes them to be very sincerely attached.'

'Then he is a most fortunate young man. He is at a time of life when, if a man chooses a wife, he generally chooses badly – and he has found that sweet young woman. If he and his family looked all around the world for a perfect wife for him, they could not have found one better!'

'You speak as if you envy him.'

'I do, Emma. In one respect he is the object of my envy.'

Emma's heart clenched. Was he about to confess his feelings for Harriet?

'You do not ask me why I envy him, Emma. You are wise. But I cannot be wise. I must tell you what you will not ask, even if I wish it unsaid the next moment.'

'Then don't!' Emma was now convinced he was going to tell her about Harriet and she did not want to hear it. 'Please, Mr Knightley! I beg you! Do not say it!'

He looked at her and said nothing. They walked on in

silence. Her arm was still through his. As they approached the house, Emma felt ashamed of her outburst.

'Mr Knightley,' she said, 'I stopped you ungraciously just now. If you have something you wish to tell me, as a friend, I will listen.'

'As a friend!' repeated Mr Knightley. 'Emma, that is a word I have no wish ... ' He stopped. Then: 'No, I will tell you. I have already gone too far to hide my feelings.'

He stopped again and looked into her face. The expression of his eyes overpowered her.

'My dearest Emma,' he said. 'For dearest you will always be, whatever the outcome of this conversation.'

Emma could not speak. She was afraid she was going to wake up from the happiest dream she had ever had.

'I cannot make speeches, Emma,' he continued. 'If I loved you less, I might be able to talk about it more. But you know what I am. You hear nothing but truth from me. I have blamed you and lectured you and you have borne it as no other woman in England would have borne it. But you understand me. You understand my feelings. So tell me, dearest Emma, speak to me if you can. Is there any chance that you could return them?'

Emma spoke – of course she did. What did she say? Just what she ought, of course.

A lady always does.

Chapter 8
The Plan

What totally different feelings Emma took back to the house from those she had brought out! She had walked out into the garden in such gloom, such wretchedness – and was now in an exquisite flutter of happiness; a happiness that she believed would be even greater when the flutter passed away.

They sat down to tea with Mr Woodhouse, the three of them together, just as they had so many times before. How often had Emma's eyes fallen on the same flowers and observed the same beautiful effect of the western sun! It had never looked as lovely as it did now.

Poor Mr Woodhouse little suspected the plans that had been made behind his back. And this was one of two serious blots on Emma's happiness: her father … and Harriet. Emma knew that while her father lived, she could never leave him. It was out of the question to marry and move away. *And Harriet – poor Harriet – how could she bear to be let down by yet another man upon whom she had set her heart?*

Emma lay awake all that night and by morning had decided upon a plan. She would write to her sister in London and ask her to invite Harriet to stay. London, with its streets and its shops and the children, might be enough to take her friend's mind off her troubles.

She got up early and wrote her letters: one to Isabella, one to Harriet. It was done. But it left Emma so very nearly sad, that Mr Knightley, walking up to Hartfield for breakfast, did not arrive too soon.

'Ever since I left you last night,' he said, 'my mind has been hard at work on one subject.'

The subject followed: how to be able to ask Emma to marry him without it affecting the happiness of her father. He knew Emma would never leave Mr Woodhouse, and he would never ask her to do so. And like Emma, he had been awake at night trying to find a solution. He had at first hoped to persuade Mr Woodhouse to move with Emma into his house at Donwell after the wedding. But he knew the old gentleman could never be removed from Hartfield. So, he had another plan which he hoped his dearest Emma would approve: he – Mr Knightley – would move to Hartfield; as long as the happiness of Emma's father depended on Hartfield being her home, then it would be his home too.

It was a perfect solution, and Emma would have been perfectly happy if not for poor Harriet. In time, she told herself, Mr Knightley would be forgotten or replaced in Harriet's heart by someone else, just as Mr Elton was.

But she feared it might be too much to hope for –
even Harriet could not fall in love with more than three
men in one year!

Chapter 9
Call Me George

Time passed on. A few more tomorrows and Harriet would be back from London. Emma had been thinking of her one morning when Mr Knightley arrived.

'I have something to tell you, Emma. Some news.'

'Good or bad?' she said, looking up into his face.

'Good, I think. Though I am afraid you may not agree.'

'Why so?'

'There is one subject, I hope only one, on which we do not think alike.'

Emma looked at him, a question in her eyes.

'Harriet Smith?' he said. 'She is getting married. To Robert Martin.'

'No!'

'It is so, indeed. He told me himself not half an hour ago.'

Emma stared at him. 'I cannot believe it,' she said. 'You cannot mean to say that Harriet has accepted Robert Martin. You cannot mean that he has even proposed to her again. You only mean that he intends to. He thinks he might.'

'I mean that he has done it,' said Mr Knightley. 'And he has been accepted.'

'Well!' Emma had never dared to hope that things could turn out so delightfully. 'You must tell me everything! How, where, when? Let me know it all.'

'It is a simple story. Robert went to London on business a few days ago and I got him to take some papers I was wanting to send to my brother. While he was there, he was invited to join the family on a trip to the circus – the party was my brother, your sister, the children ... and Miss Smith. Robert accepted, and in the course of the evening found an opportunity to speak to Harriet alone. He asked; she accepted. It is the oldest story in the world.'

Emma's heart was too full for speech. Mr Knightley misunderstood her silence.

'Emma, my love,' he said, 'I remember your disapproval when we talked of this before, but – '

'No,' she said. 'I was wrong, I was foolish. I do not disapprove – I most sincerely wish them happiness. I am just so surprised. I had reason to believe that Harriet was ... even more determined against him than she was before.'

'Well, you know your friend best,' said Mr Knightley. 'But I should say she was a good-tempered, soft-hearted girl who is not likely to be very very determined against any young man who told her he loved her.'

He was right. Emma realized that Harriet had

never really stopped liking Robert Martin and that his continuing to love her had proved irresistible. Such a heart! Such a Harriet!

She laughed. 'Upon my word, Mr Knightley, I believe you know her quite as well as I do.'

Mr Knightley's mind had moved on to other matters.

'"Mr Knightley",' he repeated thoughtfully. 'You have always called me Mr Knightley. And I am so used to it that it does not sound too formal any more. Yet – I want you to call me something else. But I do not know what.'

'I remember once calling you "George" about ten years ago. I did it because I thought it would annoy you. But as you made no objection, I never did it again.'

'And cannot you call me "George" now?'

'Impossible!' said Emma. 'I can never call you anything but Mr Knightley. Never!'

But she did.

The wedding day was fixed, and within a month of the marriage of Mr and Mrs Robert Martin, Mr Elton was called on to join the hands of Mr George Knightley and Miss Emma Woodhouse.

The wedding was much like other weddings and Mrs Elton, when her husband told her about it, thought it all extremely shabby and very inferior to her own: 'Very little white satin, very few lace veils – a most pitiful business!'

But the small group of true friends who witnessed the ceremony all agreed on one thing: it was quite, quite perfect.